DEATH
ON TOAST

" The page in my book said: '*Deadly poisonous. Common in beech woodland. Looks similar to the edible mushroom.*' But lightly fried in butter and garlic, mixed with tomato and there it was. Cheap, nourishing and just a tad fatal when mixed with another special ingredient from our garden. I'd better not say what, just in case a nutter reads this and tries it out.

After all, there are some weird kids about. **"**

More great reads in the SHADES 2.0 *series:*

Witness *by Anne Cassidy*
Shouting at the Stars *by David Belbin*
Blitz *by David Orme*
Virus *by Mary Chapman*
Fighting Back *by Helen Orme*
Hunter's Moon *by John Townsend*
Animal Lab *by Malcolm Rose*
Tears of a Friend *by Jo Cotterill*
Danger Money *by Mary Chapman*
A Murder of Crows *by Penny Bates*
Doing the Double *by Alan Durant*
Mantrap *by Tish Farrell*
Coming in to Land *by Dennis Hamley*
Life of the Party *by Gillian Philip*
Plague *by David Orme*
Treachery by Night *by Ann Ruffell*
Mind's Eye *by Gillian Philip*
Gateway from Hell *by David Orme*
Four Degrees More *by Malcolm Rose*
Who Cares? *by Helen Orme*
Cry, Baby *by Jill Atkins*
The Messenger *by John Townsend*
Asteroid *by Malcolm Rose*
Space Explorers *by David Orme*
Hauntings *by Mary Chapman*
The Scream *by Penny Bates*
Rising Tide *by Anne Rooney*
Stone Robbers *by Tish Farrell*
Fire! *by David Orme*
Invasion *by Mary Chapman*
What About Me? *by Helen Orme*
The Real Test *by Jill Atkins*
Aftershock *by Jill Atkins*
Mau Mau Brother *by Tish Farrell*
Sixteen Bricks Down *by Dennis Hamley*
Crying Out *by Clare Lawrence*
Gunshots at Dawn *by Mary Chapman*
The Calling *by Penny Bates*
Ben's Room *by Barbara Catchpole*
The Phoenix Conspiracy *by Mary Chapman*
The Team with the Ghost Player *by Dennis Hamley*
Flood *by David Orme*
Flashback *by John Townsend*
No Good *by Helen Orme*

DEATH
ON TOAST

John Townsend

SHADES 2.0
Death on Toast
by John Townsend

Published by Ransom Publishing Ltd.
Radley House, 8 St. Cross Road, Winchester, Hampshire SO23 9HX, UK
www.ransom.co.uk

ISBN   978 178127 638 9
First published in 2014

Freddy's Blog
Saturday
11.30

I'd never seen a dead body before. Apart from Denzil when I was six. Mind you, he was a hamster. This is different.

I shouldn't really be telling you this. There again, you probably won't believe any of it. But I'm going to tell you the lot, just as it happened. Then the world will know the truth from my blog.

I've called it *Fredblog Dot Com*. The dot com bit is clever, I reckon. You'll soon see why.

Three *fast facts* about me:

1. I'm 14, but I'm not giving away my birthday – just in case.
2. I'm Freddy and I live in the UK, but no clues where – just in case.
3. I've just seen a dead body. Human. For real. Not a splattered corpse in a horror movie. I've seen enough of those. No, this is very fresh. Still warm. But I'm not telling you who. Not yet – just in case.

This isn't one of those boring blogs about the weather, collecting stamps or what I've had for breakfast with a photo of a bacon butty. No, my blog's different. I can't wait to find out what you think.

Some of what I'm going to write might shock you. I'm going to put everything in. The whole lot. Surprises. Secrets. Big-time confessions to make your toes curl ... or even drop off. I've got to tell it as it is.

I only hope my English teacher doesn't see this. It was Mr James who told us to write a blog to 'get a sense of audience' and to get feedback. If you ask me, 'feedback' sounds like throwing up. Back comes the feed.

'Doctor, I can't help vomiting.'

'Ah, that's just a bit of feedback.'

Mr James didn't find that funny. He wouldn't find this blog funny, either. If he reads this, it would really let the cat out of the bag.

Talking of cats, my Mum once said I was like an old tomcat. I don't think it was from the smell in my bedroom, but because I don't need much looking after. I keep myself to myself. I've always been a loner and that's always suited me just fine.

In fact, Mum told Dad they ought to have a cat-flap fitted for me (or a Freddy-flap) so I could come and go without bothering them. In the end, they settled for a front door key, which I've had since I was nine.

For five years I've been coming and going whenever I like, because they're never here. Kids like me are called 'latch-key kids' in America. They get special help. I just get Cuppa-soups.

I reckon Cuppa-soups smell better than they taste. If I was the manager of Cuppa-soup Ltd, I'd bring in three new flavours:

1. Big Mac, fries and blue-cheese dressing
2. Fish and chips with mushy peas (with

a splash of vinegar that won't curdle)
3. Mushrooms on toast (with garlic, parsley and a hint of grated special bits).

I don't want you to think I'm some sort of mad teenage freak. It's just that I've always been a bit different.

There again, I'd never say we were a normal family. Nothing weird. Posh parents who are always busy – never at home. Me by myself. Always.

The best way to describe our family is 'three people who share nothing but the same fridge'.

The thing is, that's always suited me. I can do just what I like. That's most kids' dream! Think what you'd do if you could do just what you liked, whenever you wanted.

The only thing is, I'm beginning to think

it's not such a big deal after all. Not now. To be honest, it's all gone a bit pear-shaped.

You're about to find out just how bad the shape of a pear can get …

Sunday
14.58

I didn't sleep last night. I watched scary movies all night in my room. I ate a whole tub of caramel ice cream with toffee chunks under the duvet.

I'm still under the duvet now. I haven't got up yet. I'm typing this on my phone as there's something I've got to tell you.

Make sure you keep it to yourself. Don't

say a word. It's just that I need to tell someone. Anyone. I can't keep it to myself any longer.

Until now I've always kept my secret in the family. Not that we're close … all wrapped up in our own worlds.

Mum and Dad have never been so wrapped-up as they are right now. To be honest, they've never had much time for me. In fact, they've never even liked me. I can't think why.

I told Mum what I felt. She carried on putting on her lip-gloss and hairspray.

'Don't be silly, Freddy. We live in a lovely country area and we've got a nice home. This is a posh house, Daddy is very rich and you've got all you want.'

I didn't say anything.

Nice house or not, my parents are never in it. For Christmas I gave them the DVD of *Home Alone*. They didn't see the joke.

'You don't understand, Freddy. You're only fourteen. We have careers to worry about. We have to work long hours because you eat so much. You cost us a fortune in food.'

That's a laugh. Food like Cuppa-soup, Pot Noodles or tins of beans. The kitchen cupboard's full of them. The freezer's crammed with boring ready-meals.

I don't know when we last had a proper meal. One of those sit-down-round-the-table jobs. They didn't even manage one of those at Christmas. I ended up having a turkey with sprouts Cuppa-soup, shared with the dog.

'We've got a big drinks do at a hotel with clients. It's vital we go. We can't take you,

Freddy. Not with your spots. You'll put everyone off their olives and dips. You'll have to stay at home and amuse yourself on your Xbox. Stay in and enjoy your presents and look after the dog.'

All I got were naff socks and manky Mister Men pants, with a year's supply of cotton-buds and a tube of face scrub. I was well mad.

Dad said they'd bring me back a present from the party. Big deal! It turned out to be no more than a Christmas cracker with a riddle in it.

> '*Question*: In your home, which room has no walls or ceiling but a very hot floor?'
>
> *Answer*: A mushroom on toast.'

I told them I didn't get it. 'Mum, what's one of those?'

'You know very well what a mushroom is,

Freddy. They're on pizzas.'

'I know what a mushroom is,' I said. 'But I've got no idea what a *home* is.'

It's great to wind up my mum. She went mad.

'Don't be so stupid, Freddy. You live in a very nice one. It cost us a fortune. And don't you forget it.'

'Oh, one of those! A home is a place full of Cuppa-soups, stressy parents who never talk or who go away for days on end.'

She glared at me and swore. I fell about laughing.

I hate Sundays. I feel so yuk.

It's windy and raining. From here I can see right down the garden. It's gross out there. Grey and cold. Just one bent flower poking up by the compost heap. All alone.

I know how it feels.

I've got Maths to do. Revision. I'm not going to do it. We've got a test tomorrow. Yet another one. I've spent my whole life being assessed.

But I don't care anymore as I'm not going to school for a few days. I'll stay at home with my DVDs. I want to watch *Killer Kids from Kindergarten*. Then I'll go online and order lots more horror movies and mega-violent computer games. Cool. They're all '18' but who's to know?

Only you.

You're not going to tell anyone, are you? You won't breathe a word. I want you to promise.

Then I'll tell you my secret.

Tuesday
00.14

I can't get to sleep. I keep hearing noises, but I know no one's here. I should be used to being in the house all by myself at night. But it's so creepy. I wish I hadn't watched *Zombie Flesh Eaters* before bed.

I've always had to spend nights alone. Ever since I can remember. The joys of being an only child in a house where they're always out. Talk about lonely. It's just as well I can go online whenever I want. I can share my feelings and they stay secret. No one knows who I am. I'm just known as *fredblog*. It's always been my username, but it means so much more now. My little joke.

Joking apart, I'm a bit of a sad case really. I've got no proper friends, only virtual ones.

I never have to type in POS to them. There's no fear of 'Parent Over Shoulder'. More like PAO for 'Parents Always Out'.

Maybe I should get some virtual parents to talk to. At least they wouldn't keep on about Cuppa-soups and worry about their looks all the time. I reckon Mum's had more face-lifts than all of Hollywood put together.

And she still looks gross, if you ask me.

Skin as lumpy as bubble-wrap. I blame her for passing on my spots gene.

I once said, 'It's good to keep things in the family, eh, Mum?'

She was well upset and phoned Kalvin. He's her 'stress nurse'. He arrives in a rusty old van to give her a leg wax and foot massage. Only when Dad's away. But I can't say any more.

Dad and I do most of the housework. She says she has to keep her hands smooth for her image. I once caught her in rubber gloves spraying bleach in the washing machine.

'Your dirty pants have been in there,' she said. I tried to tell her my boxer shorts weren't nuclear waste.

For some reason, I disgust her. I usually have to wash my own clothes. I said to her once, 'Mum, you're the only woman I know who needs the sat-nav to find the tumble dryer.' She didn't smile.

Dad told me, 'You'll understand one day, Freddy. Your mother has a stressful job. She and I have to look tip-top and be seen in all the right places. That's why I go away a lot. The golf course is my website.

'And it's vital for your mother to spend every Saturday at the hairdresser's so she can look her best for work. Image is key. We have to wear the right labels. Our faces must be upfront and out there.'

I didn't argue. I just squeezed one of my spots and dabbed on some cream.

All they think about are their careers. Since she got her GNVQ in retail, she's set to become a big noise in underwear at Marks and Spencer. She travels the world buying knickers. I've often wished I could take her back and get a better fit – with a bit more time.

Dad's got a top job at Esso. Or so he keeps telling me. At a big dinner party he went on and on about how excellent he is in oil. So I piped up, 'So are sardines, but they don't brag about it.'

I was sent to bed without so much as a sniff of a Cuppa-soup.

Dad's problem is he's such a know-all. He has to be right all the time. A proper bighead.

And he can never see the funny side. Like that time when I was ten and he took me to one side.

'Your mother says I need to talk to you, Freddy. About sex.'

'That's OK, Dad. Just relax. What do you need to know?'

He went mad. I was grounded for making fun of him in 'such a childish way'. So I pointed out that's what I was – a child. It's my job to be childish. It's what I do best.

I've never forgiven him for his outburst at Open Day in the middle of the school hall.

'Come along, Freddy. Pop to the toilet for a "make-sure" before we go.'

Everyone stared. I could have died.

And why is it adults are always telling you not to do things they do themselves?

'Don't bite your nails!'

He does it all the time when he's driving the Jag. And if I say anything, it's always those four words every adult says when they're cornered ...

'Because I said so.'

'Mum, why can't I stay the night at Robert's?'

'Because I said so.'

The real reason is, 'Because we'll have to have him back here and I don't like him.'

If I had friends, they'd be banned. They might leave a spec of dust on the new carpet. I'm never allowed in the front room unless I take my shoes off and check my socks with a microscope.

I told her, 'I bet I'd never have to take off my shoes in Robert's house. His mum wouldn't mind.'

'No, I don't suppose she would,' she snapped. 'Because she's not our class.'

When she's not at work, Mum goes away on 'Beauty Weekends' or 'Spa Evenings'.

When I asked her if they were to get rid of her double chin, she stormed out the house. Off to see Kalvin.

It was the time she went all sulky after

'going up a size'. One millimetre on her hips and it's a world disaster. Sweets aren't allowed in the house. Mars bars are banned.

'Don't eat chocolate. Not between meals.'

When else is there, for pity's sake?

'Keep off the chips. They'll upset your spots.'

I tried to explain that I eat them, not rub them in my face.

Then she said to me, as she stood in her Marks and Spencer pink silk bath robe, after stepping off the scales with a scream, 'Freddy, why is it you eat so much and stay so skinny? I hate you. I really hate you!'

I think she was only joking, but I gave her one of my scary stares with a twisted grin. Just like the serial killer in *High School Bloodbath*. Then I croaked in my best psycho voice …

'Not as much as I hate you, my dear … '
You should have seen her face.

Thursday
14.34

I've taken the day off again. I hate school. I
just can't face it at the moment. I blame
Mum and Dad. They've been getting to me
lately.

I often speak as if they're still here. I try to
talk of them in the present tense. It seems
best. But they're not here any more. They

won't come back now. They've gone away for good.

It's a month now. A whole month of living on my own and running their affairs all by myself.

And I love it! Sweets when I like. Shoes in the front room. Feet on the sofa. Pants left where I like. More money than I want. Any adult DVD I care to watch, whenever I want. Extreme horror and violence all night. Life's a dream. Not a Cuppa-soup in sight.

It happened so quickly. I made up my mind when I came in the door and found yet another note telling me to open a tin of beans and be in bed by ten thirty with a Cuppa-soup.

'We're away till Sunday. Make sure you wipe the sink in the bathroom after doing your spots – and leave the toilet seat DOWN.

Keep the kitchen tidy and soak your pants in bleach.

Don't forget to walk the dog, dig the garden and cut the lawn.

Stay out of the front room!'

Something snapped inside.

A voice in my head said, 'Why do you put up with all this? Get rid of them, my dear ... '

And when a voice says that, you just have to listen.

I'd always fancied running my own affairs – taking charge of my own life.

Well, now I can and no one's the wiser. I can run this place better then they did. When I'm eighteen it'll all be OK, anyway. No more lies.

If only Miss Finch knew it was her who gave me the idea.

Her Biology lessons are usually grim, but my eyes lit up that day she held up a poster of the Death Cap Fungus.

I just couldn't help thinking of Mum – and her weakness for garlic mushrooms. From a packet, of course.

The seed was sown in my little mind.

That weekend I searched the woods at the end of the lane. There were masses of them, poking their deadly heads up through the fallen leaves. The page in my book said: *'Deadly poisonous. Common in beech woodland. Looks similar to the edible mushroom.'*

But lightly fried in butter and garlic, mixed with tomato and there it was. Cheap, nourishing and just a tad fatal when mixed with another special ingredient from our garden. I'd better not say what, just in case a nutter reads this and tries it out.

After all, there are some weird kids about.

So, spread over a frozen pizza then popped back in its box in the freezer – this was a topping to die for. Just the job. Ready and waiting. Delicious and deadly.

To be honest, I didn't think it would really work. Not so fast, anyway.

What upset me most was Mum giving some to the dog. Within minutes Sadie was slumped in the laundry room. It wasn't one of our better mealtime conversations, either.

Not that it was a proper family meal. She was doing her paperwork at the table

the note to say they were ill, but Miss Finch asked tricky questions. Still, I've always had her round my little finger so it's no big deal. Not all parents attend anyway.

In fact, it wouldn't surprise me if half my class has done the same as me. It's probably quite common.

I might go to school tomorrow. I'll see. I don't want them getting awkward and asking too many questions.

The thing is, I like it at home on my own in the day. I watch gross DVDs on the wide-screen with the sound turned up full. Then the screams echo all round the house.

Call me sad, but it beats school. And I can lose hours when I'm online.

I've got to log off now. I need to answer the phone. It's been ringing all day.

Time for some more lies …

Wednesday
22.48

Marks and Spencer won't leave me alone. They don't like the 'Uncle in New Zealand' story.

They insist Mum's got to do a major PowerPoint presentation in Dublin. Something about 'Underwear for the Fuller Figure'.

Her line manager says he smells a rat. He

says he's going to call round. I haven't slept since.

Miss Finch upset me a bit, too. She said she wanted a 'quiet word' after the lesson.

She came straight out with it. Why didn't I have any friends? She said I was a loner and seemed a bit odd. She's noticed that even Robert doesn't talk to me now.

So I used a bit of my boyish charm and gave a wink … with a twisted grin. Then my stare. That seemed to make her back off.

When I got home from school I checked Mum's emails. I think my plan worked. I'd sent her boss a message telling him just what she thought of him.

As an added extra, I said she was running away with her secret lover at Head

Office. There haven't been any more texts or emails since, so I reckon I'm safe. I hope so.

But then came the bombshell. Just when I thought I was off the hook, who should appear on the doorstep? Miss Finch!

I was gobsmacked, but I kept dead calm. I was churning inside, but I didn't let it show. I was just in the middle of heating a curry and pouring a beer.

She started by saying she was concerned. She called it a home visit from my caring form teacher. She asked all kinds of questions, like had I done my Biology homework on fungi and rotters?

I told her she had no need to worry on that one. I said I'd done quite a bit of my own research. I could tell she was impressed.

Of course, I had to ask her into the house. I didn't care about her shoes, even though they were muddy.

'I parked down the track,' she said. 'I had no idea you lived out here in the wilds.'

'Yes,' I smiled. 'Quite a classy area. Not even any neighbours for a lad to annoy.'

I even let her into the front room. She left a mark on the carpet but I said it didn't matter.

'We're very relaxed in this house,' I said. 'Mum and Dad are so relaxed they're horizontal! Let me show you round. I can tell you'd like a peep.'

It felt weird showing my teacher round the crime scene. But it was kind of thrilling, too. I can't explain it – but I got a real buzz. After all, I've kept the house tidy. Nothing to hide. Apart from a few DVDs that I hid under a cushion.

'What a posh kitchen. All these gadgets. I'd die to have a kitchen like this.'

'Really?' I said.

Then she came out with it. What I'd been dreading all along. Could she speak to Mum or Dad?

'They'll be quite a while yet,' I said. 'Things are very busy right now. Mum's away. She's in Dublin.'

Miss Finch gave me a look, then went on and on about understanding boys like me.

I could talk to her at any time. Was I in trouble? Was I upset?

'After all,' she said, with a strange stare, 'I know there's something wrong. I looked in the garage window on my way in. Both your parents' cars are in there, aren't they?'

I told her we're a three-car family. Dad was out in the BMW. That shut her up – but not for long. That's when she came out with her trump card.

'I popped into Marks and Spencer after school.'

'Really?' I said. 'Would you like a cup of tea while you wait?'

'They told me she'd left, Frederick. All a bit strange. Something about New Zealand. Something about a man at Head Office. Something about an enquiry.'

That's when I found my drama lessons came in handy. I had a little cry. Just for effect. Nothing much. Just to put her at her ease.

I wiped my nose on the tablecloth and said, 'Mum and Dad have got such a lot on top of them at the moment.

'I'd like to explain everything to you, but you mustn't tell anyone. I'd prefer to keep it in the family.'

'You can trust me, Frederick.'

'What if someone at school asks you why you came here?'

She looked quite hurt. 'No one knows I'm here, Frederick. I'm here because I care, not because anyone sent me. I haven't even told my partner where I am.'

I smiled. 'I'd feel better if you joined me for a meal. I could talk to you better then.'

She paused.

'Of course. I understand. If that would help. Can I do anything?'

'No, it's almost ready. I've just got to pop something in the soup and that's it.'

'It smells great. What sort of soup?'

'My favourite,' I said, adding the last ingredients. 'Cream of mushroom.'

'I love mushrooms,' she said. 'Especially wild ones like those.'

'That's good,' I said. 'Because I'll give you some more on toast. Extra tasty. With garlic and something special from the garden.'

'That would be lovely,' she smiled. 'I'm very impressed by your Food Tech skills.'

While they sizzled in the pan, she looked out of the kitchen window. Down towards the compost heap.

'What a super garden. It must be rich soil.'

'Yes. A lot of body in it. Lots of worms. I've done a bit of digging since your lesson on maggots. That compost heap is full of them now. I'll take you down there later. Before it gets dark. After I've told you everything. After I've spilled the beans.'

I did, too. Baked beans over the mushrooms … while I ate a ham roll and told her my terrible secret. She soon finished her soup, but didn't seem to hear what I was saying.

She ate her mushrooms on toast in silence before giving an ugly stare.

'I hate these mushrooms,' she grunted.

I gave my evil laugh. The one from *Psycho Chainsaw*.

I croaked, 'Not as much as I hate you, my dear … '

She didn't seem to see the funny side.

I'd never heard a teacher groan before. It wasn't nice, I can tell you.

She was still gurgling as she went in the wheelie-bin.

By the time I'd trundled her down the garden, there wasn't a sound to be heard.

Apart from the first thud of the spade …

Friday
04.37

I've not been well. Quite bad, in fact.

It's nothing I've eaten. That's because I haven't eaten a thing for ages. Not since the ham roll when Miss Finch called.

To be honest, I've hardly slept since. I dread this time of night. I feel sick in my bones.

I have to admit, I had a bit of a panic after I buried the evidence. Miss Finch's car was the problem.

I had to act fast to get rid of it. Well, I couldn't leave it there down the track, could I? A red soft-top VW is a bit obvious, after all. Especially with Year 9 Biology books and a bag of cream cakes on the back seat.

It was after midnight when I plucked up courage to turn the key and start the engine.

A gentle purr drifted through the mist. I let off the handbrake, pressed down the clutch and crunched into first gear.

The car shot forward and jolted along the track, as I tried to work the clutch and change gear. I didn't turn on the lights – just in case. There was enough light from

47

the moon for me to see where I was going. It wasn't far.

The car skidded up the track through the trees. A badger waddled just ahead as the engine whined. I turned off through a clearing and slid over the mud. Up to the top of the old quarry.

It was very dark there, so I flicked on the headlights. Mist swirled in the beam. An owl flapped away into the night. My heart was pounding like a drum.

I pressed a button, the roof quietly slid back and I stared up at the stars. Moonlight spilled across the Biology books on the back seat. The night was cold and deathly still as I pulled on the handbrake, switched off the engine and got out of the car.

I stepped forward very slowly – towards the edge. My toes jutted over the cliff-top.

I peered down through the darkness to the deep, shimmering lake … glinting silver beneath the moon.

I took a deep breath, let off the handbrake, flicked off the lights, ran to the back bumper and pushed as hard as I could.

Slowly the car moved forward, until the front tyres rolled over the edge with a crunch. I fell into the mud as the car juddered and scrunched before hurtling out into space with what sounded like a sigh. It seemed to hang in mid-air, then glide in slow motion.

Suddenly I gasped. Shrill music blared up from below. It drifted up from the dark shape falling through the night towards the lake.

Miss Finch's mobile. Whoever would be calling her at his time?

I should have switched it off. I should

have checked.

I swore ... just as the night filled with a roar as the car plunged below the silver spray.

The echo finally died, the water swirled and the lake closed over ... before shimmering peacefully once more. As smooth as glass, with a shivering moon.

I turned, gave a sigh and walked back down the track towards home.

I felt strangely calm. Relief, like the mist, swirled around me. Only the moon knew my secret now.

Or so I thought.

Monday
02.51

I slept for two days and nights. I think.
   I've lost all track of time.
   I blame Mum's sleeping pills. They
knocked me out a treat. That's till the
scream woke me.

It was my own scream, as it turned out.
That was really scary.

Then I heard voices. Mum and Dad's. They sounded like they were calling from the compost heap.

I keep seeing Miss Finch slumped in the laundry room. I hear groaning coming from the wheelie-bin.

I feel Sadie lick my hand whenever I shut my eyes. I know it's all in my mind but it's really weird.

To be honest, I'm scared.

I'm too scared to watch DVDs any more. I've got a box set of *Psychic Devil* to see, but I just can't face it. I feel like there's a DVD constantly running in my head. But I can't turn it off. The croaking voice with the evil laugh never stops.

I bet I won't sleep tonight. It will take me a while to check my blog. The secret I've just written.

I don't regret what I've done. Not really. Apart from the voices in my head.

I keep shaking, too. Despite the sleeping pills, I can't rest.

It's always there in my sleep – the smell of garlic mushrooms. The bedroom fills with the stench and I always wake feeling sick.

The nightmares are all the same, too. I'm driving a red car as it falls through the night with a mobile ringing somewhere in the mist … before a hand grabs me.

Screams echo all round the house.

Someone out there knows the truth.

A voice on the mobile whispers my name. It says the police can trace a phone exactly. They know where the car is. They're watching me.

That's why I wake screaming. That's what makes me sick. The reason I can't eat.

They say a worry shared is a worry halved. Telling someone can be a great help.

That's very true because I can't keep my secret to myself any more. It's killing me. Eating away at my bones.

That's why I've done the blog. I had to. I think I feel a bit better already. You see, you're helping me.

I just need to tell someone – to get it off my mind.

I'm not stupid. I've changed all the names in this blog to be on the safe side. I'm not really called Freddy. Even Sadie isn't her real name. I'm not totally mad.

And of course, you haven't got a clue who I am. All you know is my username –

fredblog.

That's the beauty of blogs and chat rooms – I'm totally anonymous. You've no idea where I live.

After all, we're always warned never to give away who we really are – so I'm not going to. The police won't know who *fredblog* is, either. It's just another *blog.com.*

That's the joke, now. Dot-com. I like to think DOT stands for Death On Toast and COM is Cream Of Mushroom. Funny, eh?

If you read this blog, I wonder if you think I did the right thing.

I'm not that bad really – am I?

At first I wasn't going to send this at all. Of course, I'll delete it all so there'll be no trace on my phone and tablet. But I'm about to click on 'post'.

That's because it's just happened. My

worst fear. It's the moment I've been dreading …

It's way past midnight. I'm still in the house alone. I'm sitting here shivering. I've been on my Xbox for hours … but now there's hammering on the front door. Drumming through my head. Thumping like my heart. Pounding though my body …

I'm not going to answer. I'm not going downstairs.

Never.

They'll have to come and get me. The blue light is flashing through the bedroom curtains. It's sweeping around the room, swirling across the screen, pulsing in my eyes.

So now I know it's over.

At last.

I'll send this and delete. Then at least someone will know the truth ... YOU.

PS

Please keep this to yourself. Don't tell a soul, will you?

Like I always say, it's best to keep things under wraps. Just like Mum and Dad always taught me. Keep things in the family. Covered up.

After all, they should know.

By the way, let me know if you want any scary DVDs. All harmless fun.

Up to a point.

Dedication

To Kit Harington.

Death On Toast began as a very long monologue which Kit first performed in Year 10 (with me playing the teacher he happily poisoned).

Thus started Kit's career of acting, stardom and villainy (well, now and again!)

Also to Toby Burchell, whose performance and mushrooms on toast in the same school drama studio years later were unforgettable

... and just a tad deadly.

Flashback

by John Townsend

Bernard has a dark secret – and he's been living with it ever since he was a child. Because, deep in the past, Bernard did a terrible thing. He killed someone. He was even seen as a hero at the time. Now Bernard lives with his nightmares. Can he face up to his past and lay his demons to rest?

The Team With a Ghost Player

by Dennis Hamley

Jacky is a brilliant young footballer, just 17 and destined to be a star. Then a vicious foul cuts him down and it looks like he'll never play again. But no one was anywhere near when he crashed to the ground. So who or what is the culprit?

Crying Out

by Clare Lawrence

London, 2115. Mack's a Grade One and he has the world at his feet. Owen is a Grade Three, the lowest you can get. Mack's a student at a top college, while Owen lives in the grime of Zone Fourteen. But their paths are about to cross, and everything is going to change. Forever..

The Real Test

by Jill Atkins

Ryan has just passed his driving test – first time, with a perfect score. He's desperate to borrow his mum's car and take gorgeous Mollie out for the evening. But Mum keeps saying no. What's her problem? What's she afraid of ... and does she know something he doesn't?